CHARLIE & MOUSE

By **LAUREL SNYDER**   Illustrated by **EMILY HUGHES**

chronicle books · san francisco

For Mose and Lewis, of course.
And for our friends in Ormewood Park,
where every day is a neighborhood party — L. S.

For Tom and Jillybean, with tough love — E. H.

Text copyright © 2017 by Laurel Snyder.
Illustrations copyright © 2017 by Emily Hughes.

Library of Congress Cataloging-in-Publication Data:

Names: Snyder, Laurel. | Hughes, Emily (Illustrator), illustrator.
Title: Charlie & Mouse / by Laurel Snyder ; illustrated by Emily Hughes.
Other titles: Charlie and Mouse
Description: San Francisco : Chronicle Books, [2017] | Summary: Charlie and
Mouse, two young brothers, enjoy a day out together, attending an
imaginary party and collecting rocks.
Identifiers: LCCN 2014026791 | ISBN 9781452131535
Subjects: LCSH: Brothers—Juvenile fiction. | Families—Juvenile fiction. |
CYAC: Brothers—Fiction. | Family life—Fiction.
Classification: LCC PZ7.S6851764 Ch 2016 | DDC [E]—dc23
LC record available at https://lccn.loc.gov/2014026791

Manufactured in China.

Design by Kristine Brogno.
Typeset in Baskerville.
The illustrations in this book were rendered
by hand in graphite and with Photoshop.

10 9 8 7 6 5 4 3

Chronicle Books LLC
680 Second Street
San Francisco, California 94107

Chronicle Books — we see things differently.
Become part of our community at www.chroniclekids.com.

Contents

LUMPS

Charlie woke up.

There was a lump beside him.

He poked the lump.

The lump moaned.

"Are you awake?" Charlie asked.

"No," said the lump. "I am sleeping."

"How can you be sleeping?" asked Charlie.

"You are talking."

The lump

stopped

talking.

Charlie poked the lump again. "Get up,"

he said to the lump.

The lump did not get up.

"Get up!" Charlie said to the lump. "Today

is the neighborhood party!"

"It is?" asked the lump.

"Yes, it is," said Charlie.

The lump turned into Mouse.

Mouse ran down the hall.

"Mom," said Mouse. "Dad!"

He opened a door.

He found two lumps.

Mouse poked one of the lumps. "Are you awake?"

"No," said the lump. "We are sleeping."

"How can you be sleeping?" asked Mouse.

"You are talking."

"I am a mom," said the lump. "I can do what

I want."

THE PARTY

"HURRAH! Today is the party!"

shouted Charlie.

"Today is the neighborhood party!"

shouted Mouse.

"Everyone will be there!" shouted Charlie.

They danced around the kitchen.

"Where is the party going to be?" asked Dad.

"It is at the playground," said Charlie.

"When is it going to be?" asked Mom.

"Now," said Charlie.

"Sounds fun!" said Dad. "I'll bring cookies."

The four of them set out.

They pulled Blanket in the wagon.

They brought cookies.

Halfway down the street, Charlie and Mouse saw Helen and Lilly and Sam.

Helen and Lilly were climbing a tree. Sam was watching.

"Where are you going?" asked Lilly.

"Today is the neighborhood party!" shouted Mouse. "Come on!"

Helen and Lilly and Sam followed the wagon.

A few houses down, Charlie and Mouse saw

Jack and Max.

Jack and Max were digging a hole.

"Where are you going?" asked Jack.

"Today is the neighborhood party!" shouted

Charlie. "Come on!"

Jack and Max followed Helen and Lilly and

Sam, who followed the wagon.

When they turned onto Woodland Avenue,

Charlie and Mouse saw Tess and Lottie.

Tess and Lottie were playing on the porch.

"Where are you going?" asked Tess.

"Today is the neighborhood party!" shouted

everyone. "Come on!"

Tess and Lottie followed Jack and Max,

who followed Helen and Lilly and Sam,

who followed the wagon.

Charlie and Mouse passed Spenser's house.

They passed Marley's house.

They passed Nora Ann's house.

Baby Sylvia rode in the wagon with Blanket.

Soon they could all see the playground.

"Hurrah!" shouted Charlie. "Soon we will be

at the party."

They got to the playground.

The playground was empty.

Nobody was there.

It was the best party ever!

ROCKS

"I wish I had some money," said Charlie.

"Yes," said Mouse. "I wish I had some

money, too."

"How can we get some money?" asked Charlie.

"That is a good question," said Mouse.

"Let me think."

Mouse thought.

"I know," said Mouse. "We will sell something."

"That is a good idea," said Charlie. "But what will we sell?"

"Let me think again," said Mouse.

Mouse thought.

"I know!" said Mouse. "We have lots of rocks. We will sell rocks."

"That is a good idea," said Charlie. "You are very smart, Mouse."

"Thank you," said Mouse.

Charlie and Mouse loaded the wagon with

their very best rocks.

They pulled the wagon

down the street.

They pulled it to Mr.

Erik and Mr. Michael's

house.

They knocked on

the door.

"Do you need any rocks today?" asked Mouse.

"No," said Mr. Erik. "We have too many rocks

already. But if you will take ours away, I will

give you a dollar."

"Okay," said Charlie.

"Okay," said Mouse.

Charlie and Mouse

took away

Mr. Erik's rocks.

Charlie and Mouse pulled their wagon to Miss

Margaret's house.

They knocked on her door.

"Do you need any rocks today?" asked Charlie.

"Heavens, no," said Miss Margaret.

"My garden is full of them. But if you will dig

them up, I will pay you a dollar."

Charlie and Mouse dug up Miss Margaret's

rocks.

They tried to pull the wagon home. It was

very hard.

Charlie and Mouse stopped to rest.

They were very hot.

They were very tired.

"Probably we need a snack," said Charlie.

"To sustain us."

"Good thinking," said Mouse.

"I wish I had some money," said Charlie.

BEDTIME BANANA

Charlie and Mouse

were in their

pajamas.

They brushed

their teeth.

"Now it is time for bed," said Mom.

"Not without a story!" said Charlie.

"No," said Mom. "Of course not. Not without

 a bedtime story."

 She read Charlie and Mouse a bedtime story.

"Now it is time for bed," said Mom.

"Not without a song!" said Mouse.

"No," said Mom. "Of course not. Not without

a bedtime song."

She sang Charlie and Mouse a bedtime song.

"Now it is time for bed," said Mom.

"Not without a banana!" said Charlie.

"A banana?" said Mom.

"We need a banana!" said Charlie.

"You need a *banana*?"

Mouse nodded. "Charlie is right," he said. "We

cannot go to sleep without a bedtime banana."

"I have never heard of a bedtime banana," said

Mom. "Is that a thing?"

Charlie and Mouse nodded. "It's a thing."

"Okay," said Mom. "Two bedtime bananas,

coming right up."

Mom brought them each a banana.

Charlie and Mouse ate their bananas.

"Now you will have to brush your teeth again,"

said Mom.

Charlie brushed his teeth.

Mouse brushed his teeth.

They climbed back into bed.

Mom turned off the light.

"Sweet dreams, little monkeys," she said.

"Good night, Mom," said Charlie.

"Good night, Mom," said Mouse.

Mom left the room.

Charlie poked Mouse. "Hey, Mouse," he said,

"Are you still awake?"

"No," said Mouse. "I'm sleeping. But what is it?"

"I was thinking," said Charlie. "Tomorrow we

should ask for a bedtime Popsicle."

"Good idea," said Mouse.

"Yes," said Charlie. "It is."

Charlie thought about Popsicles.

He started to feel sleepy.

He turned over.

There was a lump beside him in the bed.

It was really a very nice lump.

"Good night," Charlie said. He patted the lump.

"I'm sleeping," said the lump. "I can't hear you."